This book belongs to

This edition published by Parragon Books Ltd in 2017

Parragon Books Ltd
Chartist House
15–17 Trim Street
Bath BA1 1HA, UK
www.parragon.com

ISBN 978-1-4748-9077-9

Printed in China

DISNEY MOVIE COLLECTION
A SPECIAL DISNEY STORYBOOK SERIES

From the Movie

DISNEY
FROZEN
MAGIC OF THE NORTHERN LIGHTS

Bath • New York • Cologne • Melbourne • Delhi
Hong Kong • Shenzhen • Singapore

A BRAVE BEGINNING

Kristoff excitedly led his friends into Troll Valley. "Every year at the crystal ceremony, Grand Pabbie honours the young trolls who have earned all of their level-one crystals," he explained. "It's a huge achievement."

With each step, Queen Elsa's and Princess Anna's curiosity grew. They couldn't wait to experience this mysterious tradition for themselves.

"They're here!" Bulda said, when she saw the group of friends. The valley burst into life as trolls rolled out to greet them.

"Kristoff!" a young troll named Little Rock shouted, running to hug him. Little Rock was set to be in this year's ceremony.

"I can't believe it's finally time!" he said.

"Can you tell us more about the ceremony?" Anna asked.

"It has to be performed during autumn under the Northern Lights. And we only have a few more days before the last night of autumn," Bulda said, before repeating an old troll saying: "Guardians of Earth know autumn lights and crystals glow so our bond may deepen and grow."

Anna whispered to Elsa, "Did you understand that?"

Elsa shrugged. "Troll wisdom can be very confusing."

Anna noticed Little Rock holding several items in his hand.
"I like your crystals," she said.

Little Rock proudly explained the meanings of each of his three glowing crystals.
"What about that one?" Anna asked, looking at one that wasn't lit at all.

"My tracking crystal," he explained. "It won't glow until I have excellent tracking skills. If I can't earn it, I can't be in the ceremony."

"But I don't understand," he continued. "I've been tracking all kinds of things, like caterpillars and insects."

"Little Rock," said Kristoff. "You need to venture out of the valley and use what you've learned. Tracking is more than just following."

But the idea of leaving the valley alone made Little Rock nervous.

"To be a good tracker you need to be fearless, be observant, and even be inventive sometimes," said Kristoff. "I know you can do it."

"I'll try," said Little Rock. "But I'm not sure –" Suddenly he gasped. "Look at those clouds! If we can't see the Northern Lights, there won't be a ceremony!"

Then he looked around for Grand Pabbie ... but the old troll was nowhere in sight. None of the other level-one trolls were there, either! "Where is everyone?" Little Rock asked nervously. "Did they forget me?"

"Don't worry," said Bulda. "I'm sure Grand Pabbie just went to find a new site where the lights are visible."

"Why don't we track him?" suggested Kristoff. "Maybe you can earn your crystal."

Little Rock's frown spread into a smile. "A REAL tracking quest? With all of you? Yes!"

"That could be a long trip," said Bulda. "You'd better take some warm cloaks so you don't get cold!" Quickly, the trolls dressed Anna and Kristoff in cloaks of moss and leaves. Elsa politely declined because she never felt cold.

As they started off, Elsa pointed out wisps of Northern Lights in the distance. "Maybe we should head that way?"

"That's what I was thinking!" said Little Rock, as he hurried to take the lead.

When the path split three ways, Little Rock froze. He looked back at his friends helplessly.

Kristoff pointed to the first path. "That goes back to Troll Valley," he hinted.

Little Rock stepped towards the second path.

"That's towards Arendelle," said Anna.

He confidently started down the third path. "This way!"

Suddenly, Little Rock stopped. "I'm picking up a scent."

"Trolls have an incredible sense of smell," Kristoff whispered to the others.

"I think it's Grand Pabbie!" Little Rock dropped to the ground and began sniffing along a trail ... straight to a hoof.

"Um, that's Sven," Kristoff said gently.

Little Rock tried to cover his mistake with a joke. "Sven! Stop standing on Grand Pabbie's footprints!"

Elsa could see that Little Rock was nervous, so she thought a story might be just the thing to ease his mind. "The Northern Lights make me think of the amazing beauty of nature," she said, as they continued up the mountain. "What do the lights make you think of, Anna?"

Anna smiled at her sister. She knew exactly what Elsa meant.

"One night, long ago," began Anna, "our parents took us to the top of a huge mountain, hoping we'd get a great view of the Northern Lights."

"We had never been up so high," said Elsa.

"Or up so late!" added Anna.

"We were playing hide-and-seek under the light of a full moon until, suddenly, these pink and green ribbons of light rippled across the sky," said Anna.

"The Northern Lights!" exclaimed Olaf.

"Yes!" said Anna. "Then we ran up a steep hill to get higher."

Elsa smiled. "Actually, I used my powers to make a staircase out of snow! It was like we were running up into the sky."

"When we reached the very top, a snow flurry fell around us," said Anna.
"Sitting there together with the lights and the stars and the glittering snow...."
"It was amazing," Anna and Elsa said together.

"See, Little Rock?" said Elsa. "New experiences may be scary at first, but if you're fearless, they can turn into fun adventures!"

As the group reached a frozen river, Kristoff reminded everyone to walk carefully. "I don't know how solid the ice is."

"Don't worry," said Little Rock. "I did complete my ice-trekking crystal. And this is definitely thick enough –" CRACK!

The ice split beneath Little Rock's feet! Anna and Kristoff grabbed him, but they struggled to hold him up because he was so heavy.

"Elsa! Remember the story? Maybe a stairway can get us across," Anna shouted.

Elsa quickly got to work. The group watched as a swirl of ice began to form into a stairway arching over the river.

They ran up the steps, but when they started to descend they heard a rumble. The riverbank beneath Elsa's stairway began to break off.

"I don't know what to do!" Little Rock cried. "I think this is a level-two crystal challenge!"

Thinking fast, Elsa waved her arms. Sheets of ice appeared and, when their fronts curled up and froze, they looked like sledges! "Jump on!" Elsa shouted.

Everyone swooshed down the steep arch.
Picking up speed, they raced down the frozen river.

As the sledges slowed to a stop, the friends cheered happily. They had made it across the river.

Little Rock smiled up at Elsa and Anna. "You saved us! I want to be fearless just like you," he said. He gave them a glowing crystal from his pouch. "You deserve to carry this."

Elsa and Anna admired the beautiful crystal.

Determined to be a fearless leader like his friends, Little Rock declared, "This way to Grand Pabbie!"

"That's back to the river," whispered Kristoff.

Little Rock spun around. "I meant this way!" he said, marching in the opposite direction. The others smiled. They were sure Little Rock would find Grand Pabbie and the Northern Lights, and get his tracking crystal to glow – even if he did need a little help along the way!

On the Trail

After making their way across the frozen river, the friends were sleepy so they stopped for a nap. But soon it was time to move on again. As the sun slipped behind the mountain, Little Rock and Olaf roused the group. "It's wake-up time!"

Anna and Elsa forced their eyes open. It didn't feel natural to get up with the setting sun.

"Let's go," said Little Rock. "We have to find Grand Pabbie." He reminded his friends that there were only two days left of autumn. Little Rock was determined to earn his tracking crystal and join in the crystal ceremony with the other level-one trolls.

With everyone finally on their feet, Little Rock confidently marched down the trail with the group following behind. "Trolls are naturally great trackers," he said.

"Very true," said Kristoff.

"I'm going to find clues," Little Rock announced. "And I'll leave no shrub unturned." He scanned the area and froze when something caught his eye.

"Grand Pabbie must have gone this way," he said, proudly holding up a broken-off branch.

Olaf rushed over. "Arm!" he shouted. "I wondered where I left you." At everyone's puzzled expressions, he explained he had lost it when he tried to shoo a bug out of his face.

Kristoff noticed Little Rock's look of disappointment and reminded him that everyone makes mistakes. "And imagine how Olaf would have felt if he had left his arm up on the mountain forever."

Little Rock brightened. "Glad I could help."

Then something in the distance caught Little Rock's eye.
He raced ahead to check it out.

"An important clue!" he exclaimed.

Little Rock held up a clumpy piece of bright-green moss.
"This is from Grand Pabbie's cloak," he said. "I'd know
it anywhere."

"Oooh! I have a clue, too," said Olaf, holding up his moss-covered foot. Elsa pointed out thick patches of the soft green plant scattered all over. "It's possible that it's just ... moss."

Little Rock looked around and saw that Elsa was right. He sighed. "This isn't from Grand Pabbie's cloak."

As they walked further up the mountain, snow appeared on the path. Anna and Kristoff discovered what they thought were troll footprints just off the trail. They called Little Rock over, but he was busy inspecting some other prints he had found.

"I think I have a real clue over here!" he shouted.

"I feel like I'm becoming a better tracker," Little Rock said as he followed the tracks to ... Sven!

Sven gave him a big lick across the cheek. Little Rock groaned and collapsed into the snow. He was starting to feel a little discouraged.

It took Anna a while to convince Little Rock to cheer up and
check out the tracks she and Kristoff had found.

"Those are Grand Pabbie's footprints!" Little Rock declared.

They followed the prints, higher and higher up the mountain. But when they made it to the very top, the tracks stopped.

Little Rock began to imagine what might have happened to Grand Pabbie. "A giant bird might have carried him off," he said frantically. "Or maybe a squirrel thought he was a delicious nut." Little Rock spun around nervously. "Or a swarm of angry butterflies could have just gobbled him up!"

Kristoff tried to calm Little Rock down. "There are no birds strong enough to pick up Grand Pabbie," he said. "Squirrels are friendly towards trolls, and butterflies – even when they're angry – prefer flowers."

Little Rock giggled. He realized he was being silly. But now Anna looked worried. A dark cloud in the sky was getting bigger by the second, and it had started to snow.

Little Rock offered to find shelter.

"NO!" everyone shouted. They were afraid he'd run off and get lost.

When the snow began to fall harder, Elsa got to work.

Elsa waved her arms and a beautiful ice shelter
appeared nearby. The friends hurried to gather
inside the magical ice dome.

"We may be here for a little while," said Kristoff as he settled down in the cosy shelter.

"How about another story?" said Little Rock. "Anyone have one to share?"

Olaf raised his twig arms excitedly. "This storm reminds me of a story I know. And it's about the Northern Lights. Do you want to hear it?"

Everyone agreed that it was the perfect time for Olaf to tell his story.

"On a very cold, very snowy night," Olaf began, "Elsa built me with her magic. I remember saying, 'I'm Olaf and I like warm hugs.'"

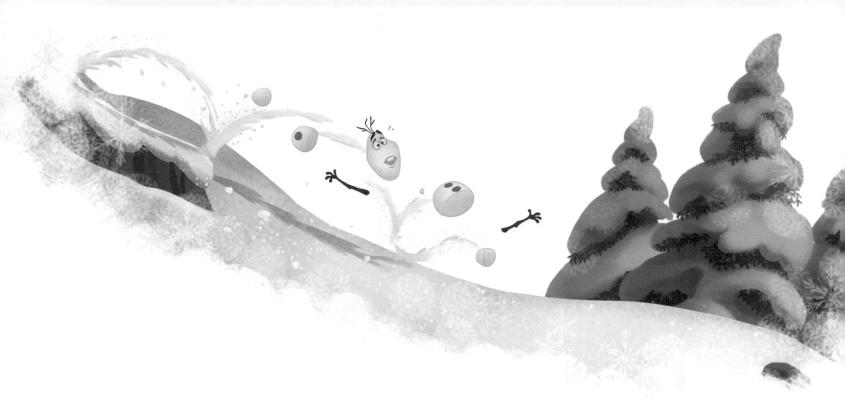

"Then I went exploring. And I ran so fast that I tumbled all over the place. I lost my head and my middle. Everything was swirling around and around. I loved it! And some of my parts collected things along the way. Two branches got stuck in my middle." Olaf waved his arms. "They became my arms. And my body picked up these little round things – buttons! And a few twigs were in my head. Hello, hairs!"

"What about your nose?" asked Little Rock.
"That came later. From Anna," Olaf said. "So anyway, when
I got to the bottom I had to work out where everything went."

"And when I was putting my final part in the right place, bright lights suddenly appeared in the sky."

"The Northern Lights!" cried Little Rock.

"Yes!" said Olaf. "How did you know?"

Little Rock giggled.

"They were green and wiggling and growing ... I watched them all night and felt so happy to be part of such a beautiful world."

"Wow," said Little Rock. "The Northern Lights shine on so many important things."

All at once they noticed that the wind had stopped. Olaf looked outside the shelter and saw that the storm had passed. The mountain was now covered in a fresh layer of thick, deep snow.

Little Rock immediately started digging. "I'm trying to uncover
Grand Pabbie's footprints," he explained.

Kristoff reminded him that the prints had stopped.

"Maybe Grand Pabbie went down the mountain," offered Elsa.
They all gazed over the steep drop, wondering how they could get down.

Little Rock grinned. He had an idea! "Remember your story, Olaf?" he asked. "Maybe we could do that."

Olaf nodded. Then he leaped over the side and began tumbling down!

Little Rock rolled into a ball and followed him.

Elsa peered over the ledge after them and gave a nod. Then she, Anna and Kristoff dived off the ledge. They laughed as they slid, slipped and rolled, racing one another down the mountain!

When they reached the bottom, Little Rock thanked Olaf for giving him the idea from his story. "Olaf," he said, "you deserve to carry my snow crystal."

Olaf gasped. He couldn't believe he was receiving such an honour!

Kristoff smiled proudly at Little Rock. "That was very observant of you, Little Rock," he said. "You realized that Olaf's story was a good way to get down the steep mountain."

Little Rock grinned. It felt great to have actually done something right! He knew he was ready for whatever came next.

LET IT GLOW

Autumn was almost gone. The chilly night air reminded Little Rock and his friends that winter was close. They had to find Grand Pabbie and get Little Rock's tracking crystal to glow before sunrise. Then he could participate in the trolls' level-one crystal ceremony.

"I'll bet there is a great clue just around the bend," said Kristoff.

Little Rock smiled. "Let's get tracking!"

Little Rock hunted for clues as the group headed up the mountain. Suddenly, he noticed a funny-looking bump under the snow.

He quickly dug down deep.

"Look!" he said, popping up with an axe and a rope.

"So that's where they were," Kristoff said. He had lost his axe and rope last spring!

"I tracked some important stuff," said Little Rock.

"You found some important stuff," said Kristoff, placing the items into Sven's saddlebag. "That's not tracking. Remember?"

Little Rock nodded. He had made the same mistake before. Tracking was a difficult skill, but Little Rock needed to work it out. Otherwise, his tracking crystal would never glow.

"But you did show inventive thinking," said Anna. "And that's one of the rules of tracking, right?"

"Yes!" Little Rock answered. "Along with fearlessness and observation."

Kristoff smiled. "Would you like to hear a story about how I was inventive, back when I was young?"

Little Rock nodded again. So, as they began hiking, Kristoff started his story.

"When I was a child, Sven and I were out harvesting ice one night. The Northern Lights were very bright and they were reflecting on the surface of the frozen lake. Sven was going crazy trying to catch the reflections.

"He carried on chasing them for a while until he finally caught one ..." Kristoff paused before adding, "with his tongue!"

Sven groaned in embarrassment while everyone else giggled at the story.

"He was completely stuck.

"So I tried pulling him ...

... and pushing him, but nothing worked.

His tongue just stretched and stretched. I reached for my ice pick, but he didn't like that idea!

"I had to come up with a better idea. I had to be inventive. So, I grabbed a teeny-tiny ice pick instead." Kristoff grinned. "And I chipped away at the ice very gently, all around his tongue, until a little circle popped out. Sven pulled the ice into his mouth and it melted. Then he was free."

"Yay!" said Olaf.

"Sven gave me a big icy-cold lick and we sat there, staring up at the colourful lights in the sky."

Little Rock laughed. "That is such a great story about the Northern Lights," he said. He wished he had a good story to share.

Suddenly, the friends spotted a trail of footprints that curved around the mountain. They followed the trail until they came to the base of a giant waterfall. There, Anna spotted a mossy cloak. Everyone agreed: it was Grand Pabbie's!

"He must have dropped it as he climbed the cliff," said Elsa.

They gazed up, wondering how they would do the same. Sven put his tongue in the rushing water. Then he did it again. Kristoff instantly understood: "He's saying that Elsa should freeze the waterfall," he explained. "Remember the story?"

"What an inventive idea, Sven!" said Little Rock.

Elsa waved her arms and the roaring water froze solid.

"Now we can climb up!" said Kristoff.

Kristoff handed Anna spikes for her shoes, and an ice axe. "I've always wanted to climb a frozen waterfall," she said.

With their gear in place, Anna and Kristoff began to scale the waterfall, digging their spikes into the ice.

"Be careful, Anna!" called Elsa.

"I can do this," said Anna, striking the ice with her axe and pulling herself up.

When Anna and Kristoff made it to the top, they threw the rope down. Elsa tied it around Sven and then helped Olaf sit on Sven's head.

"This is so much fun," said Olaf, holding Sven's antlers as they slowly started to rise up the waterfall. Once Sven and Olaf reached the top, they all hoisted up Little Rock.

But before they could throw the rope down again, Elsa had used her magic to build stairs!

When they asked why she hadn't done that in the first place, she explained. "You were so excited to climb the waterfall. I didn't want to spoil anyone's fun."

They all agreed: it was a lot of fun!

"Kristoff and Sven," Little Rock said, "because you were so inventive with the waterfall, you deserve to carry my water crystal."

Little Rock took one of the glowing crystals he'd already earned out of his pouch and handed it to them. Kristoff promised to keep it safe.

From the top of the waterfall they followed the trail as it climbed higher and higher. Soon the air became thick with fog, and although Little Rock was nervous, he kept going.

When they reached the mountain peak, a figure appeared in the mist.

Little Rock excitedly ran over and threw his arms around it.
"Grand Pabbie!" he exclaimed.

Kristoff cleared his throat and gestured towards the real Grand Pabbie.
Little Rock was confused. He looked at the moss-covered rock he was
hugging and then back at Grand Pabbie.

"I found him!" he exclaimed, running towards Grand Pabbie and
giving him a giant hug. "I tracked you!"

"Hello, Little Rock," said the kindly old troll.

Little Rock anxiously pulled out his tracking crystal and his face fell ... it was still dull!

"I bet there's just something wrong with the crystal," Kristoff said.

"Yes, there must be something wrong," agreed Anna.

"No, that's not it," sighed Little Rock. "I have something to say...."

"I'm just not very good at tracking." Little Rock held up the dull crystal and sighed. Then he explained that he would never have found Grand Pabbie without his friends. "If anyone here has earned a tracking crystal, it's all of you. Not me. I needed you, my friends, to get here."

Suddenly, Little Rock's tracking crystal started to glow!

"Look!" said Anna, pointing at the shimmering crystal.

"But I didn't earn it," said Little Rock.

Grand Pabbie nodded. "Actually, you did. You worked out what it takes to be a good tracker." For Little Rock, that meant understanding that he needed help from his friends. And that realization made the crystal glow!

Just then, the other young trolls came out of hiding, cheering, "Hooray for Little Rock!"

Grand Pabbie and the trolls had been waiting for Little Rock to find them and earn his final crystal. Now it was time for the crystal ceremony to begin.

As Grand Pabbie called for all the young trolls to gather around him, Little Rock looked shyly at his friends. "Oh, I need my other crystals now," he said.

Little Rock's friends had been keeping his other crystals safe – just in case he lost them on the journey. Kristoff gave back the water crystal. Then Anna, Elsa and Olaf handed over the crystals Little Rock had earned for learning how to be fearless and observant.

With the glowing stones in his hands, Little Rock joined the other young trolls around Grand Pabbie.

As Grand Pabbie lifted his arms into the air, all the trolls raised their crystals. The Northern Lights reflected the colours of the crystals, and the lights bounced back into the sky slightly brighter. But not as bright as Grand Pabbie had hoped.

"Mind if I try something?" Elsa asked.

Elsa waved her arms and her magic curled into the sky, creating a giant snowflake. It sparkled as it turned, reflecting the Northern Lights back into the sky and all around them!

Olaf hopped with excitement. "It's a rainbow!" he gasped.

Elsa and Anna's dresses shimmered, too.

"Well, now," said Grand Pabbie. "That is so much better!"

Thanks to the young trolls, the Northern Lights were shining strongly again. And everyone knew what the bright lights meant:

Little Rock had succeeded in his quest!